Littlest Pet Shop

What's Your MOOD?

By Ellie O'Ryan

SCHOLASTIC INC.

New York Toronto London Auckland Sydney
Mexico City New Delhi Hong Kong Buenos Aires

ISBN-13: 978-0-545-07906-8
ISBN-10: 0-545-07906-3

Littlest Pet Shop is a trademark of Hasbro and is used with permission.
© 2009 Hasbro. All Rights Reserved.

Published by Scholastic Inc. SCHOLASTIC and associated logos are trademarks and/or registered trademarks of Scholastic Inc.

12 11 10 9 8 7 6 5 4 3 2 1   9 10 11 12 13/0

Printed in China
First printing, January 2009

My Many Moods

How are you feeling today? Sweet like a kitten? Playful like a puppy? This book will help you identify all the moods you might be feeling—whether it's wacky, worried, or whimsical. So just turn the page for tons of things you can do to inspire the moods you want and to express all of your many moods!

Meet Your Moods

There are many different moods and feelings—and plenty of words to describe them! If you're having trouble thinking of the right word for your mood, take a peek at this list.

happy
joyful
silly
goofy
giggly
excited
confident
cheerful
friendly
LOVING
LOUD
eager
hopeful
outgoing
playful

shy
withdrawn
quiet
curious
impatient
bored
mischievous
antsy
THOUGHTFUL
sweet
dreamy
imaginative
motivated
lucky

sad
blue
ANGRY
mad
grumpy
jealous
ENVIOUS
lonely
depressed
hurt
lost
betrayed
emotional
MISERABLE
worried

Mood of the Day

Keep track of your moods by writing them down in a mood book. You don't have to write much—just a sentence or two about how you're feeling and what made you feel that way. (Of course, you can always write more if you want.) All you need is a pen or pencil and a notebook (or even just some pieces of paper stapled together to make a booklet). Every night before bed, get in the habit of writing down the date and your mood. You can use the list of moods and feelings on the previous page to pick the right word.

playful

Personality Quiz

What's your personality type—and how does it affe
your mood? Take this quiz, then turn the page to fin
out what your answers say about you!

1. It's a rainy Saturday afternoon, and you don't have any plans. You decide to:
   a) snuggle up with your favorite pet and a good book.
   b) hang out with your best friend.
   c) invite a bunch of friends to your house for a pizza party.

2. There's a new girl in your class at school. You:
   a) introduce yourself and invite her to sit with you at lunch.
   b) smile and wave.
   c) wonder if she's shy about meeting new people, too.

3. What kind of after-school activity suits you best?
   a) Drama club—I like to be the center of attention!
   b) Sports—teamwork is where it's at.
   c) Art lessons—I like to work quietly by myself.

4. Your perfect birthday celebration would include:
   a) going out to dinner with your family and your best friend.
   b) a party with all the kids in your class and a karaoke machine.
   c) a small sleepover at your house with your closest pals.

You have to do a big project for school. You would rather:
a) work on it by yourself.
b) work on it with a partner.
c) work on it in a group.

Spending time in a big group of people leaves you feeling:
a) excited and energized! You can't think of anything more fun.
b) tired and shy—sometimes it's exhausting to hang out with so many people at once.
c) happy and content, as long as there are a few people in the group you can really connect with.

When you chat with your friends, you:
a) put a lot of thought into anything you say—even if it means you don't say much at all.
b) say the first thing that pops into your mind—you have opinions, and you want them to be heard!
c) keep up with the conversation, listening and talking in equal measure.

Personality Quiz Scoring

1.
a) 1
b) 2
c) 3

2.
a) 3
b) 2
c) 1

3.
a) 3
b) 2
c) 1

4.
a) 1
b) 3
c) 2

5.
a) 1
b) 2
c) 3

6.
a) 3
b) 1
c) 2

7.
a) 1
b) 3
c) 2

If you scored **7–11** points, your personality type is introvert.

That means you tend to be more shy and quiet than outgoing and loud—think quiet bunny instead of squawking parrot. Some of your favorite activities are things you do alone, such as reading or surfing the Web. In general, introverts would rather hang out with one or two close friends than a large group of people. If you respect your introvert tendencies, you'll be happier in the long run.

If you scored **12–16** points, your personality blends parts of the introvert and the extrovert types.

Sometimes you appreciate time to yourself—like a content cat. Other times, like a bird in a flock, you want to hang out with your many friends! Listen to your heart and make sure that you nurture both parts of your personality.

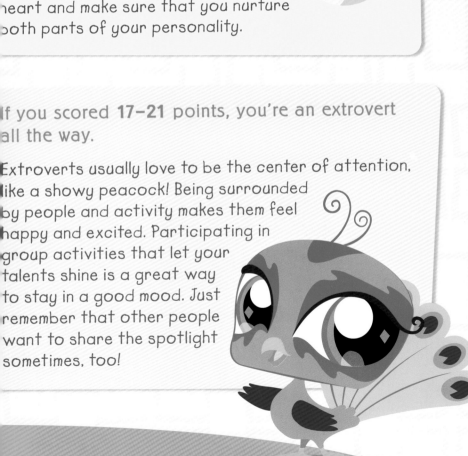

If you scored **17–21** points, you're an extrovert all the way.

Extroverts usually love to be the center of attention, like a showy peacock! Being surrounded by people and activity makes them feel happy and excited. Participating in group activities that let your talents shine is a great way to stay in a good mood. Just remember that other people want to share the spotlight sometimes, too!

Moods of Many Colors

Lots of different things can affect your mood—including the colors around you! Some color words are even used to describe feelings. For example, "seeing red" means that you're angry, while "feeling blue" means that you're sad. Check out this chart to learn how colors can affect emotions.

RED: Being around the color red can give you energy. It will actually increase your heart rate! But if you're feeling tense, upset or angry, red can make those feelings more powerful.

ORANGE: Like red, orange can make you feel more energetic and active. It can also stimulate your creative side.

YELLOW: Yellow is a bright, happy color that can help you feel more optimistic and cheerful. It might even improve your memory.

GREEN: Most people will feel more relaxed when they are surrounded by the color green. If you're tense, turn to green!

BLUE: Blue is the most calming color of the rainbow—but some shades can also feel sad or cold.

PURPLE: Purple is good for encouraging your imagination. It's considered the color of luxury and royalty. Pick purple when you feel indulgent!

Color My Mood

Now that you know how colors can affect your emotions, use them to your advantage!

Plan your outfit according to your mood—wear yellow if you're studying, or green if you're feeling nervous about something.

Decorate your room in your favorite color. Then hang different colored pieces of poster board on the wall when you need a little color-therapy.

Looking to inspire a certain mood? Try painting your fingernails the color to match. When you look at your hands, let the color work its wonders!

Plant different colors of flowers in your yard (or in flowerpots in your house). When they bloom, the colorful flowers can boost your mood.

Good Mood Food

Did you know that the food you eat can affect your mood? It's true! A healthy diet is good for your body—and good for your mood, too.

Mood Boosters

Protein Power
Foods with lots of protein can help you have more energy! Ea[t] foods such as eggs, dairy products, tofu, nuts, beans, fish, or meat to make sure you're alert all day long.

Calming Carbohydrates
Stressed out? Foods rich in carbohydrates (or "carbs") will hel[p] you feel more relaxed. Good sources of carbs include fruit an[d] whole-grain foods such as bread, pasta, crackers, and cereal—so grab one of these choices for a snack that will help you chill out!

Mood Busters

Sugar SOS
Craving something super sugary, such as a candy bar or soda? Watch out—the sugar rush you're seeking will leave you feeling down in the dumps later!

Caffeine Crash
A caffeinated drink can give you a short-term burst of energy— but once it wears off, you'll feel even more deflated.

Eating a balanced diet, with lots of fresh fruits and vegetables, whole grains, and lean protein, will give your body and your brain all the tools you need to tackle whatever comes your way!

Mood Munchies

These easy, *yummy* snacks will leave you grinning!
Always ask an adult to help you in the kitchen.

Smiley Snack Mix

Make this snack mix with lots of different ingredients.
Pick your favorites or try something new each time.

Ingredients:

- 1 cup nuts (a protein booster to give you energy)—try peanuts, almonds, cashews, and/or walnuts
- 1 cup dried fruit (a natural sugar that will brighten your mood)—try cranberries, raisins, and/or apricots
- ½ cup shelled sunflower seeds (these contain selenium, a nutrient that can balance your mood)
- 2 cups granola
- ½ cup semisweet chocolate chips (a bit of chocolate can make you feel happier!)

Mix all ingredients in
a bowl thoroughly.
Store in an airtight
container or plastic bag—
and grab a handful whenever you're
hungry and your mood could use a boost!

Smooth Mood Smoothie

A drink of this frosty banana-berry smoothie will help you keep your cool! This recipe makes enough for two servings.

Ingredients:

- ½ cup vanilla yogurt (full of protein for added energy)
- 1 cup milk (more protein)
- ½ banana (a good source of calming carbs)
- ½ cup frozen berries (berries are packed with vitamins)
- 2 tablespoons honey (a natural sweetener that will give you energy)
- ½ cup ice

Put all the ingredients in a blender and blend until smooth. Then drink it up while it's cold!

Get a Move On

Lift your body, lift your spirits! It's been proven that exercising for as little as 10 to 15 minutes a day can help to decrease sad or nervous feelings. Exercise can also help you sleep better.

Exercise for All Seasons

You can get moving in rain or shine! If the weather is nice, exercise outside by:

playing team sports

Jumping rope

Dog-walking

Running

BIKING

HIKING

If it's raining cats and dogs, move your workout inside:

Push-ups

Sit-ups

Jumping jacks

DANCING

Swimming

Yoga

Mad or Sad?

Many types of bad moods come from feelings of sadness or anger. Take this quiz to see if you respond to unpleasant situations by feeling sad or by getting madder than a hornet. Then find out how to tame your bad mood tendencies!

1. Your brother dropped your photo album in a puddle. You're:
   a) outraged! He's *always* trashing your favorite things!
   b) heartbroken. Your favorite pictures are ruined.

2. After waiting around all afternoon for your best friend to call, you find out that she went to the movies with some other kids and didn't invite you. You:
   a) are angry! You decide not to speak to her until she apologizes
   b) have a good cry and watch a sad movie all by yourself.

3. Oops! You forgot to study for a quiz and you get a grade that much lower than you're used to. You feel:
   a) really mad at yourself. You *know* you could have done better, only you'd remembered to study!
   b) incredibly disappointed in yourself. That little mistake is going to eat at you for the rest of the day.

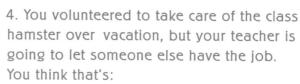

4. You volunteered to take care of the class hamster over vacation, but your teacher is going to let someone else have the job. You think that's:

a) ridiculous! You feel mad at your teacher *and* your classmate.

such a shame. You were really looking forward to taking care of the hamster.

coring

ount up the number of A's and B's.

you picked mostly A's, you get mad first and ask uestions later! It's fine to feel angry sometimes, ut don't let it eat you up inside. Try to count to en and take slow, deep breaths. When you're eeling calm, try to solve your problem without using nger-driven actions such as yelling or name-calling. you picked mostly B's, sometimes you slip into adness easily. Everyone feels sad once in a while, ut don't let sorrow dampen your whole day. Play ome happy music, call a friend for a chat, or ay with your favorite pet. When you feel appier, your problem might not even eem so bad!

Art from the Heart

The tips on the next few pages will help you use your creativity to express your emotions— whatever they may be!

Mood Collage

Feeling sad? Angry? Overjoyed? Grab some simple supplies and make a collage to match your mood. Always ask an adult' permission before beginning any craft project.

You will need:
Poster board or heavy paper, such as cardstock
Scissors
Decorative paper, such as construction paper, tissue paper, origami paper, colored foil, or wrapping paper
Old magazines
Decorative items, such as pictures, ribbons, buttons, and/or bea
Glue
Markers, colored pencils, or paint
Glitter

1. Choose a theme.
2. Use the poster board as the base for the collage. Cut interestin shapes out of the decorative paper. Don't forget to use colors an textures to express your mood. For example, a collage about ang might include scratchy, rough-textured paper and a happiness-themed collage might include shades of sunny yellow and sparkling glitter.
3. Use magazines to look for pictures that reflect your mood. A collage about loneliness might include an image of a deserted street. You can cut out words that express your mood, too!

Look around your room for decorative items to add to your collage. Don't limit yourself to paper—if you can glue it to the poster board, you can add it to your collage!

Start assembling your collage. Take the time to play with different arrangements of the paper, cutouts, and other items before you use the glue.

Once you decide on the best design for your collage, use the glue to attach all the pieces to the poster board.

When the glue is dry, use the markers, colored pencils, or paint to add some final decorations. If you feel sparkly, add some glitter!

Finally, hang your mood collage somewhere special. You can even share with your family and friends how you felt when you made it.

Mood Music

Picking the right music to match your mood can help you feel better if you're feeling low . . . and if you're already feeling good, let music boost your spirits even higher!

Feeling	Music to Match
Sadness	If you want to wallow with some sad music for a while, that's okay. Just make sure you end your listening session with something bright and upbeat, so that you don't stay sad for too long.
Anger	Ready to rage against the world? Pick some loud, screechy songs to listen to—then get up and dance out your anger! Burning off those bad feelings through movement will leave you feeling calmer.
Happiness	When you're happy, it can feel like your heart wants to sing! Pick out some of your favorite tunes and sing along with them.
Relaxation	Want to maintain that mellow mood? Then pick a calming, soothing melody to go with it!

Art from the Heart
(continued)

Write It Out

Sometimes there's no better way to express yourself than to write about what you're feeling—and why you're feeling that way. So don't hesitate to grab a pen or pencil and a piece of paper and let those words pour out of your heart!

Jump into Journaling

Writing in a journal can be the key to keeping track of your moods and feelings. If you get writer's block, start by tackling one of these topics—just fill in the blank with whatever emotion you're feeling and then see where your writing takes you.

- What happened to make me feel so _____?
- What do I want to do when I feel _____?
- What makes me feel better when I feel _____?
- When was the last time I felt _____? How did I handle it?
- Do I feel _____ a lot? Why or why not?

Fun with Fiction

Sometimes writing about your own feelings and experiences can be tough. If journaling about your life isn't appealing right now, try writing about someone else's experiences! Imagine a character that has similar feelings and explore different ways for the character to handle them.

If you can't think of a way to begin your story, try one of these starters—and have fun!

- Julia had never felt so surprised in her life. She still couldn't believe that her best friend/parents/dog/cat had _____.

- There was no way that Madison could fall asleep—not when she was feeling so _____. In just a few hours, she was going to _____.

- "Yes!" yelled Ellie as a huge grin spread across her face. She felt like celebrating. After all, it wasn't every day that her puppy _____.

- Samantha was shocked to find out that _____.

- Never in Nora's wildest dreams had she expected to feel so _____.

Chase the Blues Away

Keeping busy can keep bad moods at bay. Turn to this list for some inspiration—and then add ideas of your own!

- Play with your pet.
- Go for a walk.
- Take a bike ride.
- **Call a friend.**
- Read a good book.
- **Start an art project.**
- DANCE +☺ YOUR FAVORITE SONG.
- make a yummy, healthy snack.
- Talk about your feelings with a trusted adult, like a parent or teacher.

Happy Box

Make a beautiful box to fill with things that make you happy. When you're feeling down, peek inside the box for a quick pick-me-up. Don't forget to ask an adult for permission before starting any craft project.

You will need:

- One shoe box (with lid)
- Wrapping paper
- Tissue paper (optional)
- Scissors
- Glue
- Markers, paint, glitter, beads, stickers, and/or buttons
- Ribbon (at least 36" long)

1. Use the wrapping paper to wrap the outside of the box. Then wrap the outside of the lid. (Make sure you don't wrap the box and lid together —you'll need to open the shoe box without tearing the wrapping paper.)

2. Line the inside of the box with tissue paper or paint the inside of the box.

3. Use the markers, paint, glitter, beads, stickers, and buttons to decorate the outside of the box.

4. When the glue, paint, and glitter are dry, glue the ribbon to the wrapping paper on the bottom of the box. Make sure the ribbon is long enough to stretch up the sides of the box and tie into a bow over the lid.

5. Finally, fill your Happy Box with things that make you happy, such as photos of your pets, lists of favorite songs, memories, books, and jokes. If it brings a smile to your face, it belongs in your Happy Box!

At-Home Aromatherapy

Want a quick way to change your mood? Believe it or not, your mood can be affected by the smells around you. It's called aromatherapy. Once you know the secrets to how scent can change mood, you can use aromatherap easily!

If you're feeling tired or sad, a whiff of citrus can brighten your mood and give you energy, too! Try smelling an orange or a tangerine to boost your spirits.

Stressed out? Look to lavender to bring feelings of relaxation your way. Lavender will also help you sleep better. Try smelling dried lavender or putting a lavender plant in your bedroom.

If you feel scattered or overwhelmed, a little pepperm can help you focus. When you need to study or do homework, try smelling a peppermint candy as you suck on it.

Sweetly Scented Sachet

A sachet is a small, scented pillow filled with dried flowers and herbs. This sachet is easy to make—and works wonders for calming your emotions! Ask an adult for permission before beginning any craft project.

You will need:

- one 10" x 10" square piece of cotton fabric
- pinking shears
- 1 cup dried flowers (try rose petals, lavender, or chamomile—or a mixture of all three!)
- small bowl
- one 12" piece of ¼"-thick ribbon

1. Cut the edges of the fabric square using the pinking shears (the pinking shears will give you a nice decorative edge— and you won't have to do any sewing!).

2. If you're using more than one type of flower, mix them together in a bowl until well combined.

3. Spread the fabric out on a table, with the wrong side facing up. Carefully make a mound of the flowers in the center of the fabric.

4. Gather the corners of the fabric together so that the flowers are contained in the center. Tie the ribbon in a neat bow above the flowers. Now you have a beautiful sachet to scent your bedroom!

Mellow Your Mood

Everyone could use a little TLC (tender loving care)—especially when life gets stressful! The next time you feel tense, try one of these easy ways to chill out.

- Massage some moisturizing cream into your hands and feet.

- **Lie down in a dark room, close your eyes, and listen to your favorite music. You can also place cucumber slices or cold, wet tea bags on your eyes for extra relaxation.**

- Pamper your favorite pet—this will make both of you feel relaxed.

- Spend some time on your favorite hobby—especially quiet ones such as reading, painting, knitting, or writing.

- Try some gentle stretches and deep breathing.

- Take a soothing bubble bath (try the recipe on the next page to make your own).

Soak Away Stress

Mix up a batch of this beautiful-smelling bubble bath—then wash away your worries in the tub! Ask an adult to help with this project.

You will need:

- ½ cup unscented liquid body soap or shampoo*
- ¼ cup water
- ¼ teaspoon salt
- 15 drops of scented oil, such as lavender or peppermint oil*
  *You can replace these with your favorite scented liquid soap.

1. Whisk together the soap and water in a medium bowl.
2. Add the salt and whisk until the mixture is thick.
3. Ask an adult to add the scented oil, then stir until combined.
4. Pour some of your bubble bath under warm running water into the tub—and enjoy the bubbles!

Moods Around You

Sometimes the people around you—your family and friends—will experience bad moods. It's no fun when someone you care about is feeling down—but you can try one of the tips below to help him or her feel better.

- **LISTEN.** You can make someone feel better just by offering to listen.

- **TALK IT OUT.** Offer feedback and helpful suggestions—but try not to be too critical.

- **PLAN A SURPRISE.** Think of something special that would cheer up your friend or relative—and make it happen!

- **SHARE YOUR LITTLEST PETS.** Spending time with animal friends can make people happier!

- **APOLOGIZE.** If you did something to hurt someone's feelings, saying you're sorry is the best way to fix the problem.

- **TAKE A BREAK.** Some people want to be alone when a bad mood strikes. If that's the case, respect your friend or relative's wishes. When her or his mood turns around, you can be ready with a fun activity to do together.

- **GE+ HELP.** If the problem is too big for you to tackle alone, turn to a trusted adult for guidance.

Remember that the people you care about are only human. If they get sad, mad, or grumpy, it's normal! Show them a little extra love and kindness, and they'll do the same for you the next time you battle a bad mood.

Have a GREAT DAY!

The next time you're feeling down, don't let your mood get the best of you. Like a rainbow that appears after a thunderstorm, a good mood is never far away! Use the tricks in this book to turn around bad moods—and make the good ones GREAT!